DAD PATROL™

To ....

From ....

First published in Great Britain 2022 by Farshore
An imprint of HarperCollins*Publishers*
1 London Bridge Street, London SE1 9GF
www.farshore.co.uk

HarperCollins*Publishers*
1st Floor, Watermarque Building, Ringsend Road
Dublin 4, Ireland

ISBN 978 0 0085 1814 1
Printed in Great Britain by Bell and Bain Ltd, Glasgow
001

A CIP catalogue record for this title is available from the British Library.

FSC
www.fsc.org

MIX
Paper from
responsible sources
FSC® C007454

My daddy is kind and considerate
to others, just like the PAW Patrol.

When we're together, everything is an adventure!

My daddy isn't afraid of anything. He always likes a challenge.

Sometimes my daddy is a bit clumsy ... But so am I!

We like playing games together. He always lets me win!

My daddy helps me through the sad times.

He always knows how to cheer me up!

When I have a problem, he helps me fix it. No job is too big for my daddy!

My daddy always knows how to save the day!

My daddy's brave and strong, just like the PAW Patrol. He always helps me face my fears and prepare for the journey ahead.

I love celebrating with my daddy.

He is so much fun. My daddy is a hero,
just like the PAW Patrol.

I love you daddy!

About my daddy

My daddy is like .... from the PAW Patrol.

Loveon daddy fromon

He helps me to ....

K meplay paw to love.

I like playing ....

.... with my daddy.

He makes me laugh when ....

I ma la loved not

I know he loves me because ...... *berth esibt*

My favourite thing to do with my daddy is ......

......

My daddy is a hero because ...... *Love.*
oo) - oo)

My daddy knows how to ...... *Lr*
la ul Sienna

This is a picture of my daddy

good boy

By PAW .... **Aged** ....